Put Beginning Readers on the Right Track with
ALL ABOARD READING™

The All Aboard Reading series is especially for beginning readers. Written by noted authors and illustrated in full color, these are books that children really and truly *want* to read—books to excite their imagination, tickle their funny bone, expand their interests, and support their feelings. With four different reading levels, All Aboard Reading lets you choose which books are most appropriate for your children and their growing abilities.

Picture Readers—for Ages 3 to 6
Picture Readers have super-simple texts, with many nouns appearing as rebus pictures. At the end of each book are 24 flash cards—on one side is the rebus picture; on the other side is the written-out word.

Level 1—for Preschool through First-Grade Children
Level 1 books have very few lines per page, very large type, easy words, lots of repetition, and pictures with visual "cues" to help children figure out the words on the page.

Level 2—for First-Grade to Third-Grade Children
Level 2 books are printed in slightly smaller type than Level 1 books. The stories are more complex, but there is still lots of repetition in the text, and many pictures. The sentences are quite simple and are broken up into short lines to make reading easier.

Level 3—for Second-Grade through Third-Grade Children
Level 3 books have considerably longer texts, harder words, and more complicated sentences.

All Aboard for happy reading!

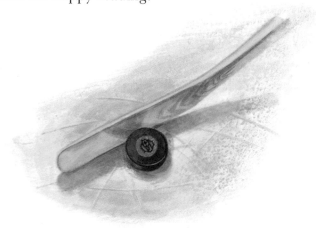

To Sudden Death Whitaker,
always there in the clutch—S.A.K.

Special thanks to Jeff Davis of the Hockey Hall of Fame and Museum.

Photo credits: pp. 15, 27, Brian Winkler/B. Bennett Studios; p.39 and back cover, B. Bennett Studios; p.48, Jim McIssac/B. Bennett Studios.

Library of Congress Cataloging-in-Publication Data

Kramer, Sydelle.
   Hockey Stars / by S. A. Kramer ; illustrated by Mitchell Heinze.
     p.   cm.—(All aboard reading. Level 3)
   1. Hockey players—Biography—Juvenile literature. 2. National Hockey League—
Juvenile literature. I. Heinze, Mitchell, ill. II. Title. III. Series.
GV848.5.A1K73   1997
796.962'092'2
[B]—DC21   97-1086
                                                                                                             CIP
ISBN 0-448-41721-9 (GB)   A B C D E F G H I J   AC

ISBN 0-448-41588-7 (pbk)   D E F G H I J

ALL
ABOARD
READING™
Level 3
Grades 2-3

HOCKEY STARS

By S. A. Kramer
Illustrated by Mitchell Heinze

With photographs

Grosset & Dunlap • New York

The Great One

California, March 23, 1994. The Los Angeles Kings are playing the Vancouver Canucks. More than 16,000 fans are at the edge of their seats. Even movie stars and the mayor have come out for this game.

All eyes are on Wayne Gretzky. Will the Kings' superstar get a goal tonight? If he does, he'll become hockey's all-time top scorer.

It's already the second period, and Wayne hasn't scored yet. But before the game, Wayne's mother told him this would be his night. He was going to break the record. As Wayne takes the ice, he's hoping she's right.

The Kings are on a power play. Wayne goes on the attack. Next to the other players, he looks small and skinny. Six feet tall, 170 pounds, he's not especially fast or strong. But no one understands the game better. That's why they call him The Great One.

Wayne controls the puck. Bending forward at the waist, he skates down the ice. His helmet looks too big, and the right side of his jersey is carefully tucked in. That's for luck. Wayne thinks that if it's loose, he won't be able to score.

Suddenly he passes. Then he skates hard toward the net. The goalie comes out to block a shot. Now there's a huge opening!

A teammate passes back to Wayne. The puck flies through the air. Using his wrists, Wayne takes the shot before the puck even lands. It's good! He's scored his 802nd goal!

The red light flashes. The crowd roars and jumps to its feet. Wayne throws his arms in the air and grins. "I did it!" he cries. His wife and his mom and dad rush out onto the ice. Every one of his teammates gives Wayne a hug.

The head of the NHL makes a speech. He tells Wayne, "You've always been The Great One. . . . Tonight you've become The Greatest."

Wayne has now racked up more points, assists, and goals than any player in history. He holds or shares 61 NHL records. Without a doubt, he's the best ever.

But people always believed Wayne would be great. At the age of two, he was already skating. When he was four, his father made a rink for him in the backyard.

As he grew older, Wayne would practice from 7 to 8:30 each morning. After school, he'd head right back to his rink. He wouldn't stop skating until bedtime, except to eat dinner.

By age ten, Wayne was breaking records. That year, he scored 378 goals in 85 games. He became a star all over Canada, where he was born. But being famous wasn't easy for him. He was shy and hated attention. His talent made him unpopular. People were jealous.

At age fourteen, Wayne was ready for junior hockey. But he couldn't join his hometown team—they didn't want him. He was just too good a player. If he were around, no one else could become a star.

Other teams didn't feel that way. But to play for them, Wayne would have to leave home. His parents agreed to let him go. He joined a team in a different city, and lived there with another family. It was a good move. Wayne was the greatest junior player of his time.

At eighteen, Wayne started skating for the NHL's Edmonton Oilers. Hockey fans everywhere had heard sensational reports about him. Could this skinny center really be that good?

The pressure was on. At every game Wayne could feel the fans watching him. Sometimes it seemed as if they were waiting for him to fail. There was no way he was going to let that happen.

Wayne went out and scored goal after goal. He became the youngest player ever to make the All-Star team. But that's not all. At the end of the season, he was the only rookie ever named Most Valuable Player. Now he's won the award nine times—more than anyone else.

Experts agree that no one plays hockey like Wayne. He's always on the move, and that makes him hard to check. Streaking behind the net, he can tell where each player will go and when. In an instant he'll pass the puck to an open teammate, or sneak in and score himself.

Wayne makes the sport look easy. He doesn't follow the puck around. As if by magic, he figures out where it's going next. He never fights—it wastes playing time. That may be how he earned points in 51 games in a row—hockey's longest scoring streak ever.

Wayne thinks his awards and records come partly from luck. So, before a game, he always puts on his uniform exactly the same way. And he's always the first player on the ice, after the goalie.

He's picky about his equipment. His skates must be a size and a half too small. The heavy, short sticks he uses can't have very much curve. In one game, he may use fourteen of them. Their weight must be just right—he can tell if a stick is a quarter of an ounce off.

Wayne's style has paid off. He's scored the most goals in a season (92), the most assists (163), and the most points (215). A great passer, he led the Oilers to four Stanley Cups.

Now a New York Ranger, this team player has made hockey a popular sport. No wonder his nickname is The Great One.

Super Mario

Mario Lemieux (you say it like this: le-mew) is crying. His doctors have just given him bad news. It's January 11, 1993, and all he wants to do is get home. The Pittsburgh Penguins' star center, he is always calm in the rink. But right now he's so upset, he can hardly drive.

Mario has just found out that he is very sick. Only 27 years old, he has cancer—the kind called Hodgkin's disease. The doctors told Mario there's a good chance he can be cured. But he can't play hockey for weeks. And to get well, he must have a special treatment—radiation.

Radiation will make Mario very tired and very weak. He'll lose weight and run a fever. Wherever the radiation hits, his skin will feel badly burned.

Tears cloud Mario's eyes. He can hardly see the road. It feels as if his life will never be normal again. What will he do if he has to quit hockey?

Mario's always dreamed of being a hockey great. Even as a child, he practiced for hours. His father packed snow on the hall carpet so that Mario had somewhere to skate.

By age eighteen, Mario was Canada's top junior hockey player. At nineteen, he joined the Penguins in the NHL.

It was hard for him to leave Canada for the United States. He barely knew English—he spoke mostly French. But that soon changed. Mario was a couch potato. He lay around at home and watched hours of TV. That's how he finally learned English, he says.

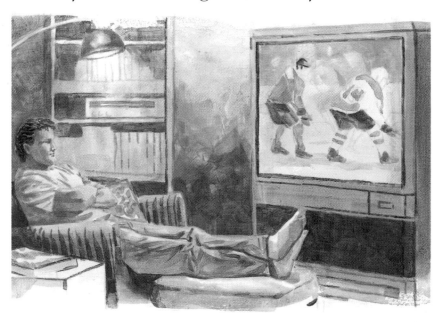

On the ice, things were easy for Mario. He got a goal for the Penguins on his very first shot. He hasn't stopped scoring since.

Named Rookie of the Year in 1984–85, Mario's won the Most Valuable Player Award twice. At six-foot-four, 226 pounds, he's one of hockey's strongest men. Always a clean player, he doesn't like to fight. With his quick, hard shot and long reach, he's led the Penguins to two Stanley Cups.

Mario's often been hurt. Yet he's always come back strong. But this is different. He's going up against cancer.

Mario starts his treatments. Soon he has no energy. His legs feel heavy. He loses his sense of taste, and must force himself to eat. Still, he keeps practicing.

He wants to try to stay in shape. As captain of the team, he means to return this year.

On March 2, he has his last treatment. That same night he and the Penguins play the Flyers. "It's been a long two months," he says. "I missed the game."

Mario's illness has lasted a quarter of the season. No one expects him to play well right away. Before he got sick, he was the league's scoring leader. Now someone

else has taken the lead. Not even the Penguins think Mario can get it back.

He surprises everyone. He skates as if he were never sick. His long, graceful strides speed him right through defenders. Even in a crowd, he skillfully passes the puck. He doesn't take shots until the last instant. That way, they're always a surprise.

In the season's last 20 games, Mario scores an amazing 56 points. The Penguins go on to the playoffs. And Mario wins the scoring title—he scored more points in 1992-93 than any other player.

It seems as if Mario has the cancer beat. But all at once he slows down. The radiation is still in his body. It's making him weak again. Then his back starts to bother him. He can barely skate anymore.

Mario has to miss most of the 1993–94 season. But his mind is made up—he's not quitting hockey. He takes the next season off and gets some rest. Lifting weights and exercising, he builds up his strength. Mario does everything he can to get healthy again.

The plan works. He roars back into the NHL. As powerful as ever, he always

checks hard. He's so strong, he can score one-handed with defenders on his back. In 1995–96, he wins the scoring title. Then he does it again for the sixth time in 1996-97.

Yet he never brags. He is quiet and keeps to himself. He's been known to hide in the bathroom after games so he doesn't have to speak to reporters.

At the end of 1997, Mario retires from hockey. He is only 31, but he's done a lot in his career. MVP a total of three times, he's the NHL's sixth leading regular scorer. He has the most shorthanded goals in a season, and holds the record for most overtime points.

In French, Mario's native language, Lemieux means "the best." Fans everywhere agree it's the right name for him.

Team Eric

October 6, 1992. Eric Lindros is
nervous. He hardly slept last night.
He's about to play his first NHL game,
and it's against the great Pittsburgh
Penguins. Eric is the Philadelphia Flyers'
rookie center. He's only nineteen years
old.

Fans are packed into the arena. Eric
knows they're studying his every move.
Canada's best junior hockey player, he's
already famous. Experts are saying he'll
be the game's next superstar.

But some people can't stand him.
They think he's a greedy snob. That's

because Eric won't play for just any team—only one that's well-known and has money.

Others believe he's nothing but a mama's boy. They say his mother makes his decisions for him. He may be big and strong, but he won't do anything without her advice.

Many fans, though, admire Eric. They feel he has the right to join the team he wants. It's a good thing, they say, that he's close to his family. After every game, the fans mob him for his autograph. He needs a bodyguard to get through the crowds.

Now Eric takes the ice. He hears both cheers and boos. Tonight, more than anything, he wants to show how good he is.

The first two periods go by. Eric has trouble staying calm. He later admits, "I panicked a couple of times." The Flyers fall two goals behind. Eric hasn't helped much so far. Is he just too nervous to bring his team back?

The third period begins. Eric looks for the puck. He wants to make a big play. He knows he's the strongest man on the rink tonight. Over six-foot-four, and 230 pounds, he can knock anyone off his skates. He's so big, one of his teammates says he "looks like an apartment building coming at you."

Suddenly Eric's got the puck! It takes him just three steps to hit full speed. He charges down the middle of the rink.

The Penguins try to stop him. Eric fights them off. No one can tell what his next move will be.

He's almost on top of the net. With his thick wrists he flicks the puck past the goalie. His shot's so hard and fast, it zooms into the net like a rocket. Score!

It's Eric's first NHL goal. Now he's got the Flyers going. They come back to tie the game, 3–3.

Eric has shown the fans that he has talent. But he still has something to prove—that he can be a great all-around player. For the next two years, he pushes himself hard. When he's not playing terrific defense, he's scoring, then scoring some more. One player calls Eric "an absolute hockey machine."

But Eric's not a machine—he has feelings. He wants to win so badly, he can't always keep those feelings under control. He loses his temper and gets into fights. He checks so hard, he leaves players dizzy—and mad. Many think he has a mean streak.

Eric sometimes skates wildly. Crashing into the boards, he hurts himself. In some games he doesn't seem to know what he's doing. Instead of helping the team, he gets penalty after penalty.

In his third season, Eric settles down. He's still a power player, but he tries not to get carried away. He thinks of the team first, and that helps him become its leader.

At twenty-one, Eric is named the NHL's youngest captain. He heads the Flyers' line, nicknamed the Legion of Doom. He can shoot the puck through a defender's legs, race past him, get it back, and score.

At the end of the 1994–95 season, Eric is named MVP. He is just twenty-two years old. When he accepts the award, he cries. For him, the MVP Award is a dream come true.

Eric started skating at three. As he grew older, he worked hard at the game. He practiced on a rink his parents made for him in the backyard. His hero was Mark Messier. (You say it like this: Mess-ee-ay.) He carried Messier's hockey card in his wallet.

On the ice, he was always sure of himself. But he never showed off. He often hid how good he was so he wouldn't make his teammates jealous.

These days Eric's a superstar. But he's still a little shy. Even now he speaks so softly, he's hard to hear.

His goals have changed, though. He's not skating to prove he's the best. He thinks of himself as just one of the team. What he wants most is to help the Flyers win the Stanley Cup.

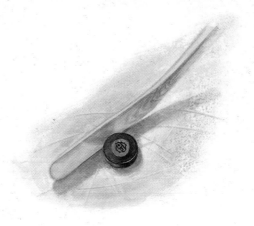

Saint Patrick

Patrick Roy (you say it like this: WAH) is staring at the net. In his mind, it's growing smaller and smaller. Soon it seems so tiny, no one could possibly score.

He skates to the crease and starts talking to the goalposts. No one's surprised—he does this before every game. Patrick calls the posts his friends and tells them they'll have a great game. He explained once, "They talk back to me, and when they say 'Bing,' I know they're with me."

Patrick is the Montreal Canadiens' star goalie. Tonight he needs all the help his goalposts can give him. It's June 7, 1993. Game 4 of the Stanley Cup finals is beginning. The Canadiens are in California to face the Los Angeles Kings. If Montreal can win, they'll lead the series, 3–1.

Patrick knows there's only one way to beat the Kings—he has to keep the puck out of the net. But this season has been a poor one for him. He's only twenty-seven years old, yet people are saying he's washed up. Fans often boo him. He thinks he might even be traded.

Patrick wants to prove he can still deliver. In the past, he's been at his best in the playoffs. He led the team to the Stanley Cup in 1986, his rookie year. When he was twenty, he became the youngest hockey player ever to win the playoff MVP. Now he wants the Canadiens to win the Cup again.

The game begins. Patrick seems nervous. He jerks his head, stretches his neck, and shrugs his shoulders.

But in fact he's calm. He can't stay still because his mask makes his face so hot.

By the end of the second period, Patrick has let the Kings score twice. He scolds the goalposts, as if it were their fault. But in the locker room between periods, he makes a promise. He tells his teammates, "No more goals."

Patrick keeps his word. When the
third period ends, the score is tied, 2–2.
In overtime, Patrick really comes through.
His stick is fast. He knocks down shots
with his glove. Whenever he makes a save,
he praises the goalposts. If he slams back
against them, he thanks them for holding
him up.

Then all at once the Kings charge the net. One player shoots. Left-handed Patrick blocks the puck. Another player swings his stick, socking Patrick. Patrick doesn't budge. He just winks at the man. Later he says, "I wanted to show him I was tough. That I was in control."

By the time the game is over, Patrick has made 40 saves. The Canadiens win, 3–2. They go on to take the Stanley Cup.

Patrick has made an amazing comeback. He's set a record in these playoffs—ten straight overtime wins. For the second time, he's named the playoff MVP. He's only the second goalie in hockey history to manage that.

Patrick wanted to be a goalie ever since he was seven. It wasn't because goalies could block shots or make the big saves. He remembers, "I liked the pads. I saw all that equipment and I wanted to wear it."

He learned to drop to his knees to make a save, then jump right back up on his skates. It's still his style. One reporter says he looks like "a jack-in-the-box."

Patrick moves around in front of the net. He knows quick reactions aren't enough to stop a shot. So he studies where players like to shoot the puck. That's how he decides where to stand.

Six feet tall, 192 pounds, Patrick's been named the NHL's outstanding goaltender three times. For four years, he had the fewest goals scored against him. In 1988–89, he played 34 games in his home rink—and didn't lose a single one. Now he's a model for all young goalies.

A friendly guy, Patrick's always signing autographs. He loves to talk and argue with his friends. When he retires from hockey, he says he might become a lawyer.

But that's a long way off. Now with the Colorado Avalanche, Patrick is the best playoff goalie in the game today. In 1996, he helped the Avalanche win their first Stanley Cup. It's hard to believe that just a few seasons ago, people were saying he was finished. Patrick has had some bad years, but fans have learned never to count him out.